Summer Wheels

Eve Bunting

illustrated by Thomas B. Allen

Voyager Books
Harcourt Brace & Company

San Diego   New York   London

Requests for permission to make copies of any part
of the work should be mailed to: Permissions Department,
Harcourt Brace & Company, 6277 Sea Harbor Drive,
Orlando, Florida 32887-6777.

First Voyager Books edition 1996

Library of Congress Cataloging-in-Publication Data
Bunting, Eve, 1928–
Summer wheels/by Eve Bunting; illustrated by Thomas B. Allen. — 1st ed.
p. cm.
Summary: The Bicycle Man fixes up old bicycles and offers both
his friendship and the use of the bikes to the neighborhood kids.
ISBN 0-15-207000-1
ISBN 0-15-200988-4 (pbk.)
[1. Bicycles and bicycling — Fiction. 2. Friendship — Fiction.]
I. Allen, Thomas B., ill. II. Title.
PZ7.B91527Su 1992
[Fic] — dc20 90-49758

B C D E F

A B C D E (pbk.)

Printed in Singapore

The illustrations in this book were done in charcoal, pastel,
and colored pencil on Canson Mi-Teintes paper.
The display type was set in Kabel and the text type was set in
Linotype Walbaum by Thompson Type, San Diego, California.
Color separations were made by Bright Arts, Ltd., Singapore.
Printed and bound by Tien Wah Press, Singapore
This book was printed with soya-based inks on Leykam recycled
paper, which contains more than 20 percent postconsumer waste
and has a total recycled content of at least 50 percent.
Production supervision by Warren Wallerstein and Diana Ford
Designed by Camilla Filancia

To Ernie, and memories of summer
— E. B.
To Yosef and his kids
— T. A.

Chapter One

The Bicycle Man fixes up old bicycles in Mrs. Pirelli's garage. Then he lets the neighborhood kids use them for free.

Summer mornings the Man opens the garage about eight o'clock. My best friend, Brady, and I are always there ahead of him, waiting. We watch him amble along the sidewalk, drinking coffee from a Pete's paper cup, eating a jelly donut from a Pete's bag.

"Early birds get the best bikes," the Man says, grinning at us as he unlocks the door.

That door swinging open is just about the best part of the day. It's dark inside and the air smells of rubber and glue and tire cement. There are thirty-one bicycles, some of them hanging from the rafters, the rest standing in racks.

There are ten-speeds, five-speeds, trail bikes, touring bikes. There are black bikes, red bikes, yellow bikes. There are two tricycles and even a tandem. More than anything in the whole world the Man loves his bikes.

He gets his check-out book while Brady and I grab our favorite machines. Mine is a twenty-inch Sting Ray with a big banana seat and hot purple paint. Brady's is a red Moto Cross with white tires.

"Gotcha!" Brady says, running his hand across the leather saddle.

These bikes are ours for the whole, long day.

We write our names and the date and time in the Man's check-out book: Brady, Lawrence, July 10, 8:05.

"Get them back here by four," the Bicycle Man reminds us, the way he does every day.

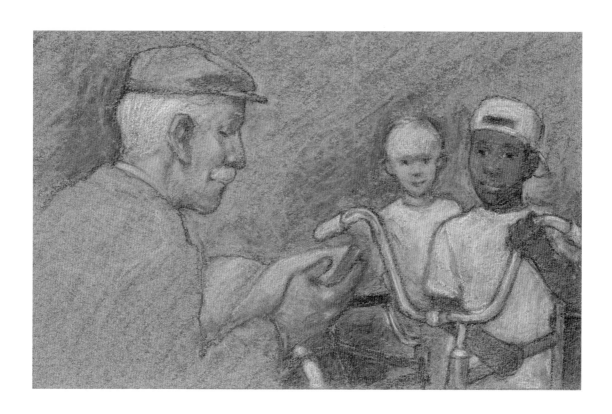

"We'll be here sooner," I say. "We have a baseball game at two."

"Ride safe," the Man calls after us.

Outside, the sky is a bright, sharp blue. We hot dog along the bike path. The sizzle of the wheels is the sound of summer.

Above us a 747 whines across the emptiness, heading for the Los Angeles airport.

I squint up at it and yell, "Race you, jet!"

We ride like crazy and get to the park gates with the jet behind us.

Brady grins at me. "Man! We're fast!"

All morning we ride in the park.

We do cherry pickers, bouncing on our back wheels, and we practice Vander rolls on the grass. Grass is softer than cement, and you have to throw yourself over the handlebars in a Vander roll.

By now we've got dirt on our T-shirts and a crowd is watching.

I showboat for a little kid in a Dodgers cap.

"How do you do that, man?" he asks me.

"He's good, that's how," Brady brags.

"Aw, it's just practice," I say. "But don't you try doing it. You're too young."

I feel fine.

This bike is as good as mine for the whole summer. If I always get to the Man's garage first. If I stay lucky.

Chapter Two

At twelve-thirty Brady and I ride back to the garage. The doors are open. Most of the bikes have been checked out and the place has an empty look.

The Man's talking to a guy about our age or maybe older. He might be twelve. The guy's wearing a torn T-shirt that says Blair Boys' Club on the front, cutoffs that droop to his knees, and old, beaten-up tennies with no laces.

"Hi, fellows," the Bicycle Man says to us. "Sign in your machines."

We do that and prop them against the far corner wall. It's the darkest spot in the garage. If some kids get here before us in the morning they might not notice our bikes.

"You mean you don't have to pay money to take one?" the new guy's asking the Bicycle Man.

"You just sign a bike out and sign a bike in," the Man says. "Easy as that."

He's munching another jelly donut and a speck of cherry red filling is stuck in his beard stubble. "Pick yourself a bike, son," he says.

Quick as a flash the guy goes to the corner and picks mine.

"Hey!" I yell. "That's my . . ." But I stop. The bike's not mine. I only think it is.

The guy's bent over turning the pedals. I hope he won't like the bike.

But what's not to like?

He wheels it across and leans it on the wall beside the check-out book.

As he's signing his name he flashes me a grin that I don't like.

"Have it back by four," the Man says. "Ride safe."

"I'll have it back." The guy grins again.

I don't believe him.

"Easy as that," he says to me as he passes.

Brady and I go to the doors and watch him walk my bike, then get on it and ride away.

"Hey!" I yell. "That's a mean machine. Take care of it, okay?"

The guy doesn't even look back.

I go to the book to check his name. He has signed Abrehem Lincoln. It's not even spelled right.

Chapter Three

Brady and I are at the garage before eight the next morning.

"Quit worrying," Brady tells me.

But I am worrying.

We spot the Bicycle Man coming along the sidewalk with his coffee and bag of donuts. I run toward him, not waiting for him to get to us.

"Did he bring it back?" I ask.

The man knows who I mean and what I mean. He looks sorry for me and shakes his head.

I'm madder than mad. My bike!

"You shouldn't have let him take it." My voice is shaking.

The Man peers at me through the coffee steam. "Why not?" he asks. "The boy wanted a bike to ride, same as you."

I can't believe what a dumb fool the Man is sometimes.

"But you shouldn't have let him take that one," I say.

"The kids pick their own bikes, Lawrence. You know that. We don't take reservations."

"Abraham Lincoln!" I say furiously. "You should have suspected."

"I'm not here to suspect," the Man says and opens the door.

Today the garage has lost its magic. The dark corner looks lonely.

Brady gets his bike and helps me pick another, a five-speed that Marta Sanchez likes to ride. She'll be missing out today.

"It's a primo bike," Brady says to cheer me up.

I'm not cheered.

We sign out.

"Be back at four," the Man tells us, the way he always does. "Ride safe!"

I glare at him. "Do we ever not come back?"

The sky is as blue as yesterday's. But these wheels have no sizzle.

Brady heads for the park but I slow and stop.

"What's up?" he asks.

"I'm going to find Abraham Lincoln," I say.

I know Brady will come with me.

Chapter Four

It's still early and the Blair Boys' Club isn't open.

Abraham Lincoln is riding my bike round and round the parking lot.

"Guess who's here?" I whisper.

We're about on him before he sees us coming. He tries to turn fast, but I pull a fork stander right behind him and Brady blocks him in front.

"Look who I found!" I tell Brady in a fake surprised voice.

Abraham Lincoln dodges around me but I grab his handlebars. "I guess we could call the police," I tell Brady in a very cool voice. I'm not sure we could since the bike doesn't belong to us. But it slows Abraham.

"We won't if you come quietly," I say. "All we want is the bike."

"Take it," the guy says.

I shake my head. "Uh-uh. You have to bring it.
You know that."

Abraham Lincoln gives me a drop dead look but
he comes.

We walk single file with him in the middle.

"You got a reason you didn't bring it back

yesterday?" I ask. "And don't say because you
planned to bring it today."

The guy shrugs. "Anybody fool enough to give
me something for nothing deserves to lose it."

"It was a lend, not a give," Brady says.

Abraham grins that ugly grin. "There's a
difference?"

I'm glad when we get to the garage.

A couple of kids are there with the Bicycle Man.

The Man's helping the Little Shrimp mend a flat tire. The Shrimp's the smallest kid who comes here. He and the Man have the bucket beside them and the Little Shrimp's saying: "I see the bubbles, Bicycle Man. I see them."

He has his little arms in the water dunking the bicycle tube.

Brady once told me the Little Shrimp doesn't have a father and that's why he hangs out with the Man so much.

Marta Sanchez is searching through the box of tire patches. She's got an okay five-speed that has a flat in front.

When she sees me she says, "All *right!* You got your bike back. Now I can have mine."

The Bicycle Man looks up. "Just fix that puncture before you go, Marta. Leave it right for the next person."

"But I didn't do it," Marta says. "This is a slow leak."

"The rule is, if it happens while you have it, you fix it," the Man tells her. Then he looks at the three of us. "Hello, Abraham. I see you came back."

"We *brought* him back. He was supposed to bring the bike yesterday," I add in case anybody's forgotten.

"Well, sign it in now, Abraham," is all the Man says.

I can't believe it. I mean, you'd expect a question at least.

Abraham Lincoln checks the bike off in the book and then he asks, "Can I take another one?"

What nerve! I'm waiting for the Man to explode, but he doesn't.

"You can," he says. "But take a different one. Lawrence was here this morning before you were."

Then he swigs his coffee and goes back to the Little Shrimp. He shows him how to mark the bad spot before taking the tube out of the water.

Abraham Lincoln takes a step closer.

"You ever do this, Abraham?" the Man asks. "You can hang around and watch if you like."

"You think I got nothing better to do?" The guy signs out and heads for the door.

I'm waiting for the Man to stop him because this is a bum bike. It's one of a bunch that's just been sitting there waiting for the Man to get to it and fix it up. The Man doesn't say a word.

Brady's the one that does.

"You've got a dud bike there," he tells the guy. "You might not even be able to ride that bike without it breaking under you. And if it happens when you have it, you have to fix it."

Abraham Lincoln growls, "Who asked you?"

And he wheels the bike out.

I go to the book to check his name.

Abrehem Lincin.

This time he's got both parts wrong.

Chapter Five

"He's not going to bring this bike back, either,"
I tell Brady.

And he doesn't.

Not that day and not the next day.

"You expected him to?" I ask the Bicycle Man on
the third day and he gives me a strange look and nods.

Unreal, I think.

The day after that Brady and I decide to check
out the Blair Boys' Club again. I've been feeling bad
about not doing it before. The Man's our friend.
This punk shouldn't be able to put one over on him.

It's after three when we get to the parking lot.
There are plenty of parked cars, but no bike riders.

"Lightning does not strike twice in the same
place," Brady says wisely.

"Let's ride around," I say. "We might spot him."

We don't see much as we patrol the streets.
People are sitting on front steps, reading newspapers.
A smoke gray cat sleeps on a window ledge.
There's a guy working on an old car. The hood

is up and a radio blasts into the hot air.

    Brady and I are about to give up when we see
a bunch of big kids. They are crowded around something, cheering.

One of the kids moves, and through the gap I see Abraham Lincoln. He's riding the Man's bicycle down some stone steps.

Thunk-clunk.

Thunk-clunk.

At each "thunk" the crowd cheers. At each "clunk" they cheer more.

Both tires are flapjack flat. Abraham Lincoln has his feet on the ground for brakes.

Thunk-clunk.

Thunk-clunk.

He looks up and sees us.

I think I was about ready to leave, quietly. But once he saw us, I couldn't.

"What do *you* want?" he asks.

Beside me I hear Brady whisper, "Uh-oh!"

I swallow. "You've got the Man's bike," I say.

"So?"

I swallow again. "You have to bring it back."

The crowd buzzes like a bunch of angry bees.

"He don't have to do anything he don't want to do," one of the biggest guys tells me.

Beside me Brady goes "Uh-oh," again. He sounds weak.

I don't know what's going to happen next.

Then Abraham says, "Stay cool. I don't care. I'll go with them."

I can't believe it. He's thunk-clunking the bike in our direction, stopping to pick up a red backpack that's on the steps.

The crowd behind him is still buzzing.

I'm wondering why Abraham's coming so easily. I'm wondering why he's coming at all. But then I stop wondering and start walking, fast. And I don't look back.

Chapter Six

Mrs. Pirelli's garage sounds like the cafeteria at lunchtime. Kids are rushing around getting bikes back, signing them in before the deadline. There's a silence when we show up. Somebody gasps.

"I brought the bike back," Abraham Lincoln tells the Man.

The kids rush to see it.

"What did you do to it?"

"Wow! What ran over it? A ten-ton truck?"

The Bicycle Man wipes his hands on a rag.

"It got trashed," Abraham tells him.

Marta Sanchez whistles a long, slow whistle. "This thing's ready for the junk heap."

The Man bends to look at it.

"It's bad, but it can be fixed. You and I have a lot of work to do, Abraham."

"I know, I know. The rule is, if I have it when it breaks, I have to fix it. Dumb rule." Abraham's eyes flicker to the Man and then away.

"Are you ready to start tomorrow morning?"
the Bicycle Man asks.
"I guess." Abraham's voice is real grouchy.

"You'll tell your mom and dad?" The Man always makes sure our parents know where we are.

"I don't have a dad," Abraham Lincoln says. "I have a mom and a grandma. No grandpa either." He sounds grouchier than ever.

But he and the Bicycle Man are looking at each other as if they understand something.

The Man curves his hand over Abraham's head. "All right, Abraham. You tell your mom. And be here early in the morning."

Abraham pulls something from the backpack. It's a greasy brown paper bag. He shoves it at the Man. "Here. I brought this for you."

The Man takes out a jelly donut. "Thank you, Abraham."

"And my name's Leon," the guy says, strutting toward the door.

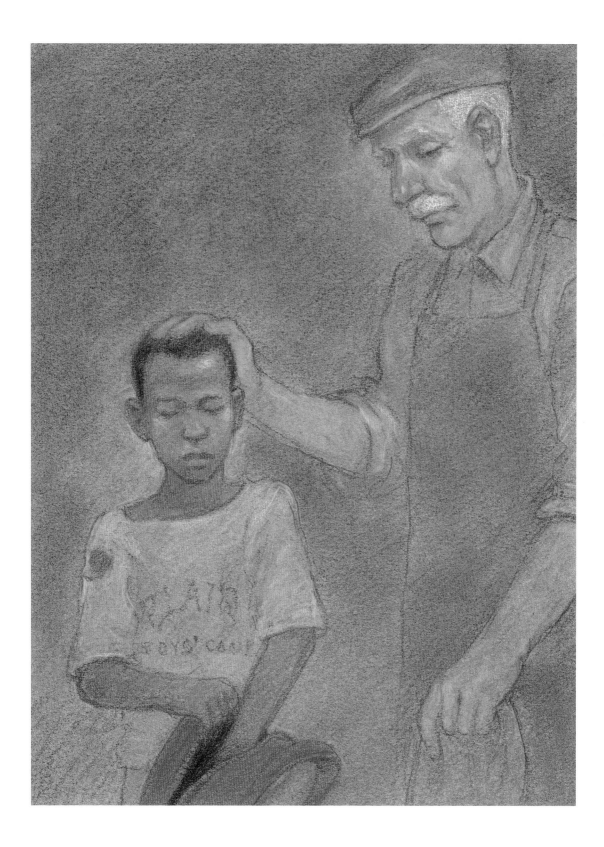

"See you, Leon," the Little Shrimp calls. The Little Shrimp's too young to know exactly what's going on.

And then we're all yelling, "See you, Leon. See you."

Leon gives a quick, surprised glance over his shoulder. Then he's gone.

The Man smiles. "You're good kids," he tells us. "Real good."

Brady's ready to burst. "But that guy trashed your bike on purpose," he says.

The Man shrugs. "I know."

Brady and I walk home.

"I think Leon wanted us to bring him back," Brady says. "I think he wanted to hang out with the Man but he was too cool to ask. He had that jelly donut all ready."

"Yeah," I say. "And I think there's something the Man likes even more than his bikes."

"Jelly donuts?" Brady asks.

That makes me laugh. "No, dumbo. Kids. Us."

I feel fine.

The sun is warm. It's summer. And tomorrow we'll be riding.